MY BOOK

FROGGIE WENT A-COURTING

RETOLD & WITH PICTURES BY CHRIS CONOVER

FARRAR STRAUS GIROUX

NEW YORK

Copyright © 1986 by Chris Conover
All rights reserved
Library of Congress catalog card number: 86-45289
Published simultaneously in Canada by Collins Publishers, Toronto
Color separations by Offset Separations Corp.
Printed in the United States of America by the John D. Lucas Printing Company
Bound by Bookbinders, Inc.
Designed by Cynthia Krupat
First edition, 1986

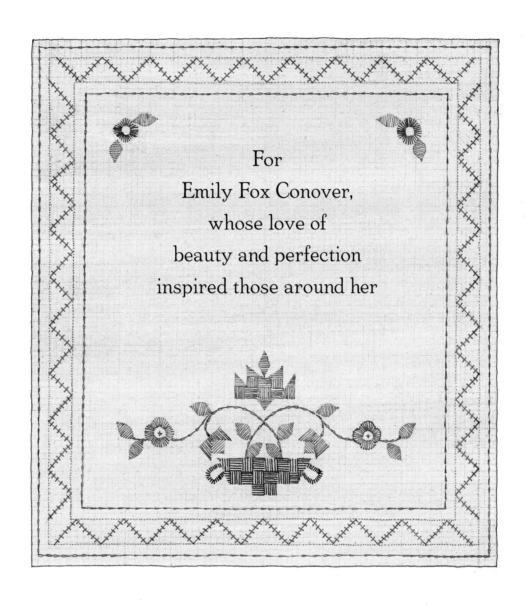

For
Emily Fox Conover,
whose love of
beauty and perfection
inspired those around her

Froggie went a - courting and he did ride,
Heigh ho! says Rowley,
Froggie went a-courting and he did ride,
Sword and pistol by his side.

He went down to Miss Mousie's door,
Where he had often been before,
Rowley, Powley, Puddin'head,
Heigh ho! says Rowley.

He got down onto bended knee,
Heigh ho! says Rowley,
He got down onto bended knee,
And said, "Miss Mousie, marry me."

"You'll have to ask my Uncle Rat
And see what he will say to that."
Rowley, Powley, Puddin'head,
Heigh ho! says Rowley.

Uncle Rat gave his consent,
Heigh ho! says Rowley
Uncle Rat gave his consent,
The moles inscribed the document.

Frog and Mousie went to town
To buy the bride a wedding gown,
Rowley, Powley, Puddin'head,
Heigh ho! says Rowley.

"Where will the
wedding party be?"

"Way down yonder
in a hollow tree."

First to come in was Ducky Drake
Carrying the wedding cake.
Next to come in were two fat bees
Bouncing banjos on their knees.

Third to come in was a big brown bug
Who jumped in the molasses jug.
The old gray goose was fourth to come in.
She picked up a fiddle and they all took a spin.

Fifth to come in was a big tom cat.
He took after Uncle Rat.

He ate up all the wedding cake
And chased the party into the lake.

Then Frog and Mousie left for France,
Heigh ho! says Rowley,
Frog and Mousie left for France,
And that is the end of this romance.

Now put the book back on the shelf.
If you want more, better sing it yourself,
Rowley, Powley, Puddin'head,
Heigh ho! says Rowley.

FROGGIE WENT A-COURTING

He went down to Miss Mousie's door,
Where he had often been before,

He got down onto bended knee,
And said, "Miss Mousie, marry me."

"You'll have to ask my Uncle Rat
And see what he will say to that."

Uncle Rat gave his consent,
The moles inscribed the document.

Frog and Mousie went to town
To buy the bride a wedding gown,

"Where will the wedding party be?"
"Way down yonder in a hollow tree."

"What will the wedding supper be?"
"Two green beans and a black-eyed pea."

First to come in was Ducky Drake
Carrying the wedding cake.

Next to come in were two fat bees
Bouncing banjos on their knees.

Third to come in was a big brown bug
Who jumped in the molasses jug.

The old gray goose was fourth to come in.
She picked up a fiddle and they all took a spin.

Fifth to come in was a big tomcat.
He took after Uncle Rat.

The cat ate all the wedding cake
And chased the party into the lake.

Frog and Mousie left for France,
And that is the end of this romance.

Now put the book back on the shelf.
If you want more, better sing it yourself.